Never Let You Go

Patricia Storms

Scholastic Canada Ltd.
Toronto New York London Auckland Sydney
Mexico City New Delhi Hong Kong Buenos Aires

The art in this book is a combination of traditional illustration using a brush, India ink and charcoal pencil, combined with digital colouring using Photoshop.

Scholastic Canada Ltd.
604 King Street West, Toronto, Ontario M5V 1E1, Canada

Scholastic Inc.
557 Broadway, New York, NY 10012, USA

Scholastic Australia Pty Limited
PO Box 579, Gosford, NSW 2250, Australia

Scholastic New Zealand Limited
Private Bag 94407, Botany, Manukau 2163, New Zealand

Scholastic Children's Books
Euston House, 24 Eversholt Street, London NW1 1DB, UK

www.scholastic.ca

Library and Archives Canada Cataloguing in Publication
Storms, Patricia
        Never let you go / written and illustrated by Patricia Storms.
ISBN 978-1-4431-1989-4
        I. Title.
PS8637.T6755N48 2013   jC813'.6   C2013-902385-2

6 5 4 3 2 1   Printed in Singapore 46   13 14 15 16 17

For my Guido, of course. I'm a lucky penguin to have found you, and rest assured, I'll never let you go.

— P.S.

I love you,
little one.

I will care for you,

and treasure you always.

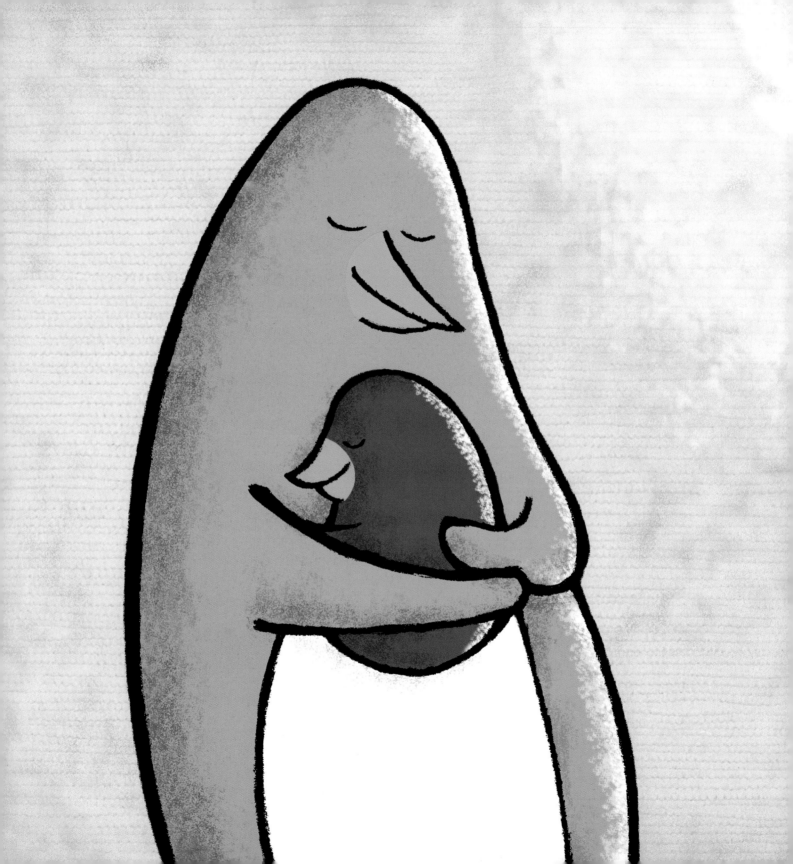

And I will never let you go.

Except when you need
to go to the bathroom.

And except when
it's time for lunch.

Or when you want to draw a picture.

But other than that,
little one . . .

I will never let you go.

Except when you have
to chase the stars.

And when you throw
a tantrum.

Or need some
quiet time.

But other than that,
little one . . .

I will never let you go.

Except when you want
to play with your friends.

But other than that,
not-so-little one . . .

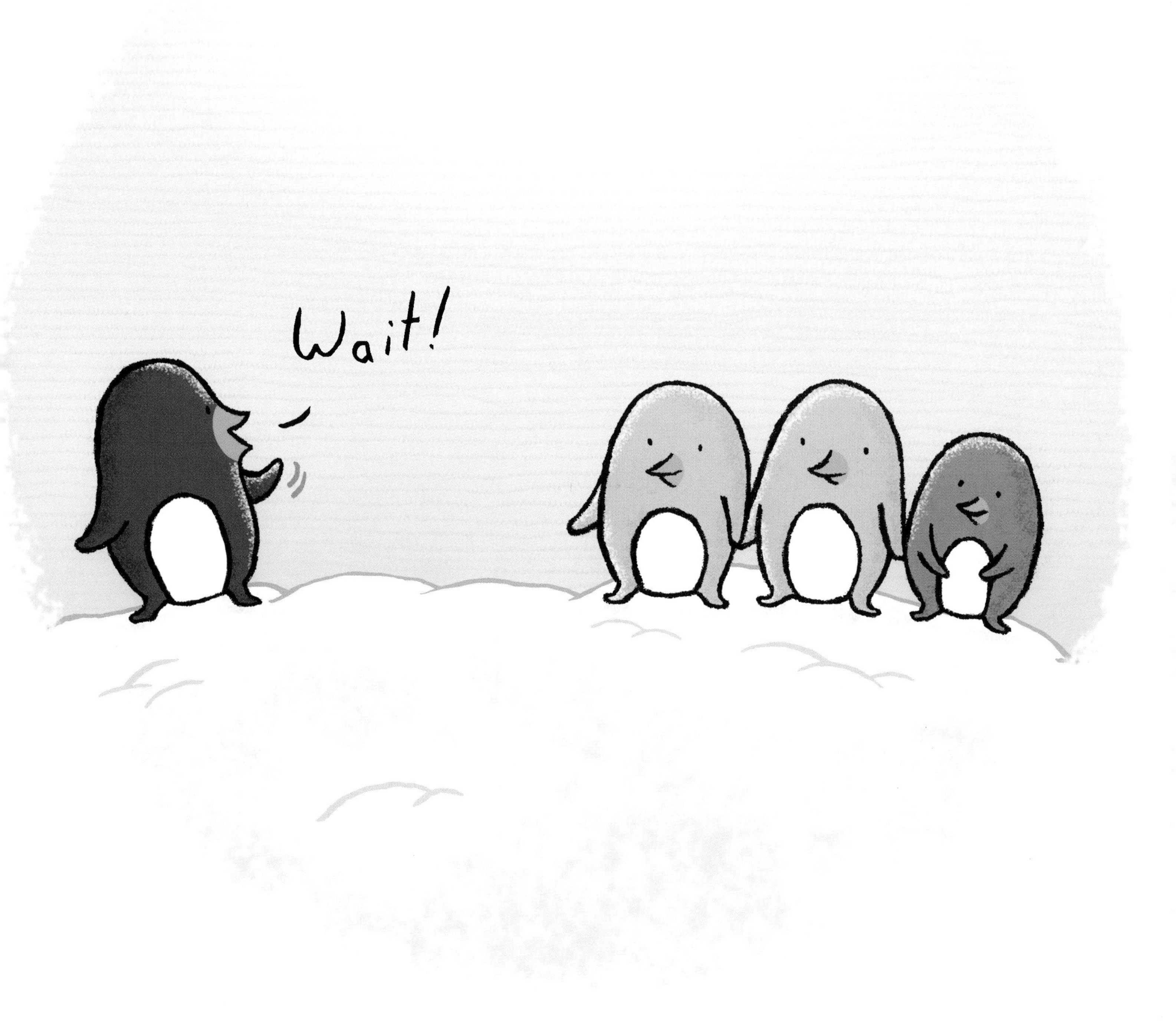
Wait!

I will never let you go.